KNOWSLEY LIBRARY SERVICE

Please return this book on or before the date shown below

D0589246

ge –

You do

ju

First published in 2004 in Great Britain by
Barrington Stoke Ltd
18 Walker Street, Edinburgh, EH3 7LP
www.barringtonstoke.co.uk

This edition first published in 2010

4u2read edition based on *Mad Iris*, published by
Barrington Stoke in 2002

ISBN: 978-1-84299-879-3

Printed in Great Britain by Bell & Bain Ltd

Meet The Author – Jeremy Strong

What is your favourite animal?
A cat
What is your favourite boy's name?
Magnus Pinchbottom
What is your favourite girl's name?
Wobbly Wendy
What is your favourite food?
Chicken kiev (I love garlic)
What is your favourite music?
Soft
What is your favourite hobby?
Sleeping

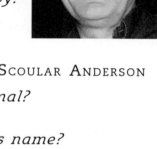

Meet The Illustrator – Scoular Anderson

What is your favourite animal?
Humorous dogs
What is your favourite boy's name?
Orlando
What is your favourite girl's name?
Esmerelda
What is your favourite food?
Garlicky, tomatoey pasta
What is your favourite music?
Big orchestras
What is your favourite hobby?
Long walks

This is for my friends in Athens:
Beth and Paris, Lydia, Phoebe and
of course, Iris (who is *not* an ostrich)

Contents

Chapter 1
Who is KJ?

The note in Ross's bag was short.

Do you want to
go out with me?
If you do, meet me
after lunch by the
conker tree K.J.

Ross went red. He folded the note and hid it in his bag. He didn't dare look up. He was thinking fast. KJ? That was the new girl – Kelly Jessup.

Kelly Jessup! Did Ross want to go out with *her?* Yes! Yes! Kelly made his legs turn to jelly and his heart thump. Kelly made ...

"Ross? Ross? Did you hear me?" said his teacher, Mrs Norton. "What do you call a triangle with three equal sides?"

"Kelly," Ross told her.

"Don't be so stupid. You can't call a triangle *Kelly*," snapped Mrs Norton.

Most of the class found this very funny. But not Katie. She waved her arm in the air.

"I think it's a great idea," she said. "We could give every shape a name like that."

"Stop being silly," said Mrs Norton. The rest of the class looked at Katie as if she were quite mad.

"Roger," Katie went on. "Roger Rectangle. That would be a good name."

Mrs Norton groaned. "A triangle with three equal sides is called ..." But just then the bell went for lunch.

They all pushed their books into their desks or bags and rushed off.

Ross couldn't wait for after lunch. Kelly Jessup was going to meet him by the conker tree!

Ross gulped down his food fast. He was longing to get away but the dinner ladies made him stay until everyone had finished. Gloria took forever to finish her rice pudding. At last he could go.

Ross dashed out to the playground but stopped some way from the conker tree. "Play it cool," he said to himself. "Just walk slowly."

Now he could see the conker tree. Yes, Kelly was there! She was grinning at something Ian Tufnell was telling her.

Ross gave a snort. Ian was an ass. OK, he was tall and good-looking and fantastic at judo. But he was a no-brain. Everyone knew that.

Ross went across and smiled at Kelly. She frowned back at him. Ross opened his eyes wide at her and nodded.

"Is something wrong?" she asked.

"Yes! No! I mean yes!" grinned Ross. "The note. Yes is the answer to your note." Ross flashed his best smile at her.

Then Ian was standing over Ross. What big hands he had! "Why don't you go and get lost?" he said.

But Ross didn't care about Ian. He was there for Kelly. He tried to look at her but Ian was in the way.

"I *do* want to go out with you!" he yelled.

Ian looked very angry. "Do you mean you want to go out with *me*?" he said.

Ross was getting nowhere. Why was Ian so stupid? "Not you – her! Kelly."

And that was when all Ross's dreams fell apart.

Kelly looked at him in horror. "Go out with you? You must be joking. I wouldn't go out with you if we were the last two people left in the world."

Ian gave Ross a hard push. "Get lost, little boy. She's going out with me."

Ross felt awful. He turned away. Kelly and Ian were laughing at him.

He felt a hand on his arm and looked up. It was Katie. She gave him a little smile.

"It's not that bad," she told him.

"It is," said Ross.

"The note wasn't from Kelly," she went on. "It was from me. I'm KJ too. Katie Jacobs."

"You!"

Katie gave him a hopeful smile. "I put it in your bag this morning. What do you think?"

Ross was very angry. He couldn't have got Kelly Jessup mixed up with Katie Jacobs! Katie, the girl with all those freckles AND she was weird.

Please say yes

Ross was about to tell her that he wouldn't go out with her if they were the last two people left in the world.

But he didn't. He was so shocked he couldn't say a word.

An ostrich had just come crashing through the school hedge.

An OSTRICH ?????!

Now the huge bird was striding across the playground. It was coming towards Katie and Ross, and it was looking at them in a nasty way.

Chapter 2
Mad Iris

Ostriches are big birds. When they are coming towards you fast they look even bigger. This one was like a huge black-and-white train with feathers.

The children in the playground ran out of its way. Mrs Norton, who was on playground duty, hid in a bush.

She was not the only one. Kelly Jessup and Ian Tufnell were in there too.

While everyone else was yelling and running away, Katie grabbed Ross and hissed at him. "Stand quite still!"

Ross did as he was told. He couldn't have run away even if he had wanted to. His legs had turned to jelly.

The ostrich stopped just one stride away from where the two children were standing. It looked at them hard.

What odd birds ostriches are! They have feathers but they can't fly. Their knees are big and bumpy. They have the most weird faces.

This ostrich stretched her neck out and prodded Ross's nose with her beak. He twitched.

"Hello," Katie said softly. "I like you."

"Don't be stupid!" muttered Ross. "You can't *like* an ostrich."

"Sssh," Katie went on, in the same soft voice. "Just speak to her nicely. And do everything slowly."

Katie put a hand into her bag as she spoke. She pulled out a chocolate bar. The ostrich snatched it from her hand and ate it.

Then the bird stuck her head into Katie's bag. It ate her ruler, her felt tip pens and a pair of P.E. socks.

"Oh!" said Katie.

"Ha, ha," laughed Ross, in a loud voice. Too loud. The ostrich lifted her head, looked at Ross for a second and bit his ear. "Ow!" he yelled.

"You asked for that," said Katie. She stroked the bird's bony head. "You're a clever ostrich, aren't you? Oh yes, and you are so good-looking. I shall call you Iris."

"You *can't* call her Iris!" Ross told her. "You're mad. *She's* mad!"

"Then I shall call her Mad Iris," smiled Katie, and it seemed a very good name for an ostrich.

Mrs Norton came out of her bush and grabbed a big broom. She began to creep up on the ostrich from behind.

"Get away from that bird," she told Katie and Ross.

"She won't hurt you," Katie said, and she stroked Mad Iris's long neck. The ostrich closed her eyes. She loved it.

But Mrs Norton knew better. They were all in danger. She had to get rid of this ostrich. She didn't want it in the school playground. She waved her broom.

"Shoo!" she shouted.

Mad Iris jerked her head up.

"You're scaring her," Katie warned.

"Shoo!" yelled Mrs Norton, and she waved her broom again.

Mad Iris took a step towards the teacher. Her head shot forward and she pulled the broom from Mrs Norton's hands. She tossed it on the ground, and with one big kick, she broke it in half and tossed it to the side.

Mrs Norton couldn't speak.

Mad Iris took another step towards her. What *was* that large, pink thing in the middle of Mrs Norton's face? Mad Iris grabbed Mrs Norton's nose in her beak and tried to yank it off.

"Ow! My dose! Let go of my dose!" yelled Mrs Norton. She waved her arms and jumped up and down.

At last Mad Iris let go and Mrs Norton sank to the ground. The ostrich stepped over the poor woman and marched into the school.

Chapter 3
Mad Iris Starts School

"Come on," said Katie. "We'd better follow her." She grabbed Ross by the arm and pulled him after her.

Mad Iris was marching up and down the corridors, poking her long beak in everywhere. She pushed her way into the caretaker's little room and snatched his sandwiches right out of his hands.

In the school office, she had a go on Mrs Perch's computer. Then she tossed the neat piles of paper all around the office.

While this was going on, Mrs Perch tried to hide in her big cupboard.

In the end, Mad Iris went into the headteacher's office. Mr Grimble didn't even look up from his desk. "What do you want, boy?" he said.

Mad Iris picked up the phone and tried to eat it. That was when Mr Grimble looked up and found himself gazing at an ostrich. The ostrich gazed back at him. Then she spat out the phone.

"Oh," said Mr Grimble. He moved slowly across to the window. He opened it softly. Mad Iris went on gazing at him.

Then Mr Grimble jumped out and ran off. Mad Iris took everything out of Mr Grimble's desk and then went off to find Katie. The ostrich liked Katie. She had chocolate in her bag.

When Mr Grimble jumped out of the window, Katie decided Mad Iris was going to be great fun.

The ostrich followed Katie into her classroom. All the other children ducked behind the tables.

"We're going to keep her," Katie told them all, and she turned to Ross. "Aren't we?"

"Yes. We are," Ross said.

Why am I saying this? thought Ross. *Why am I agreeing with Katie Jacobs? She's mad! I don't even like her!*

"You can't keep an ostrich in school," said Kelly Jessup. She was hiding behind Ian Tufnell.

Then Ian Tufnell astonished Ross by saying that he thought it was a great idea to keep an ostrich in school.

And Kelly Jessup astonished Ian by hitting him. "It's a stupid idea," Kelly told

him. "Katie's weird. Anyhow, the teachers will never let you keep her. I bet they are phoning the police right now."

And she was right. Mr Grimble and the teachers were all in the staffroom. They had locked the door.

Mr Grimble put down the phone and turned to his staff. "It's all right," he said. "The police know all about that bird. It escaped from an ostrich farm. The keepers are on their way to the school right now. We shall soon get rid of it."

Outside the staffroom door, Ross's friend Buster listened at the keyhole. They were going to get rid of their ostrich! He hurried back to the classroom to tell the news.

"We've got to save her. What shall we do?"

"We must find a safe place to hide her," said Gloria. "Somewhere with plenty of room for an ostrich."

No-one spoke. Then Mad Iris made a rude noise and a mess on the floor.

"Urrgh! That's disgusting!" cried Ian.

"She doesn't know any better," said Katie.

Mad Iris seemed to agree with her because she now tried to eat Katie's hair.

"GET OFF!" Katie slapped the bird's head. Mad Iris began to eat Mrs Norton's felt tip pens. "Stop it, you idiot!" said Katie.

"I know what!" cried Ross. "We could put her in the boys' toilets, and then it won't matter if she does a poo."

"You can't put an ostrich in a toilet," said Kelly. "She's too big."

Ross went red. "I don't mean *in* the toilet itself – in one of the booths. No-one will look in there."

"He's right, you know," grinned Katie. "Well done, Ross!"

Ross gave her a big grin.

"Ooooooooooh!" went the class, while Ross turned even redder.

Chapter 4

Anyone Want an Ostrich for Dinner?

Mad Iris liked the boys' toilets.

First of all, she pulled the toilet roll off the holder and unrolled it.

Then she wrapped the paper round the pipes, round the toilet bowl, round Ross's head, and round Buster's legs.

Then she tossed the roll over the top of the open door. Everyone thought this was very funny.

Mad Iris's next trick was to pull the toilet chain. The chain came off and Mad Iris ate it.

Katie gave Mad Iris a long, stern look. "You've got to stay here and not make a sound. Do you understand?"

Mad Iris lifted one huge foot and put it in a toilet pan. Katie lifted it back out and wagged her finger. "None of that," she said. "You must be good."

Just then Buster came rushing down the corridor.

"There are some men coming!" he yelled. "Lots of them!"

The children could hear the wail of sirens far off. It was getting louder. Some police cars and a fire engine drove into the playground. Did they think that the ostrich was going to set fire to the school?

Then a big, dark truck appeared. It stopped and some men in black jumped out.

"They've got guns!" said Ross. "They're going to kill our ostrich."

They saw Mr Grimble saying something to the men. They could hear every word through the open windows.

"She escaped from our farm yesterday," one of the men told him.

"What are you going to do?" asked Mr Grimble.

"These stun-guns fire a drug that will put her to sleep. After that, we'll take her back to the farm. She's going to be killed anyhow. They all are. We send the ostrich meat to the supermarkets. It tastes lovely!"

One of the men grinned at Mr Grimble and smacked his lips.

Mr Grimble did not want an ostrich in his school, but he was not at all happy about the men's plan.

"We'll have to move all the children out before you go into the school," he said. "And don't tell the children what you plan to do. It will only upset them."

But it was too late. The children knew, and they were already very upset.

"Now what do we do?" wailed Gloria. "If we all go outside, there will be no-one to look after Mad Iris."

They could hear their teachers calling for them. One by one they went back to their classes. Still no-one had thought of a plan.

The children were all led outside. Soon the school was silent and empty.

At least it was *almost* empty.

There was an ostrich in a toilet booth plonking one foot in and out of a toilet pan.

And hiding in a cloakroom, with their feet showing beneath some coats, were Ross and Katie.

The men in black picked up their stun-guns and marched into the school.

Chapter 5
Trouble in the Toilets

Ross knew Katie was scared. He found her hand and held it. She clung onto him and didn't let go. *Will she get the wrong idea?* thought Ross.

Here he was, hiding under some coats, with a girl clutching his hand and an ostrich stuck in a toilet booth. What a mess!

Katie and Ross looked out. They couldn't see anyone but they could hear loud voices some way off. It would not be long before the men in black came their way.

There was a terrible banging from the toilet. Ross dashed across to see what was going on. Mad Iris had found out how to put the toilet lid down. And up. And down. And up again. *Bang bang bang bang!*

"Stop it!" hissed Ross. "The men will hear you!"

Mad Iris stopped. First she tried to eat the buttons on Katie's shirt and then she had a go at Ross's ears. "Ouch!" said Ross.

Katie smiled.

"It hurt!" said Ross. He was angry.

"Shall I kiss it better for you?" asked Katie.

"No!"

Then the smile vanished from Katie's face.

"Sssh! I think someone's coming this way."

Ross softly closed the toilet door and went out into the corridor.

Next moment he flung himself back inside. Someone *was* coming! A large man was marching down the corridor checking every room, one by one!

Ross dashed back to make sure the ostrich was hidden. Her feet could just be seen through the gap between the door and floor, but there was nothing he could do about that.

"Stay very still. Don't say a word," said Ross to Katie. "We're going to hide in the next door toilet, OK?"

Mad Iris gazed at these odd children. Why did they talk so softly? What was going on? She would wait and see.

Ross and Katie went into the next door toilet booth. Ross put down the toilet lid softly and stood on it.

"They mustn't be able to see our feet," he said. Katie stepped up after him. She started to laugh.

"Now what?" asked Ross.

"What would Mr Grimble say if he found us in here?"

How come I'm stuck in the boys' toilets with this crazy girl? Ross thought.

He peeped over the wall at Mad Iris. At least *she* was being a good girl for once.

The man out in the corridor was big. He had a big, round chest and a big, round face like a burger. He gave some big burps as he went down the corridor, checking the rooms. He had his stun-gun in his hand, ready to fire.

"Is there anyone in here?" asked the big man.

The children heard a door bang as it was flung open. "No-one in *that* room!"

Is there anyone in *here?*" the man went on. "No-one in there either."

Bang went another door.

The door to the boys' toilets crashed open.

"I'd better check all the booths," said Big Burger Man.

Ross held his breath and Katie shut her eyes. The door of the toilet at the far end was opened.

"Nope," muttered Big Burger Man.

The next door opened.

"Nope," said Big Burger Man.

He opened the third door and found himself staring at an ostrich.

"Ha! Got you!" cried Big Burger Man, and lifted his gun.

Chapter 6
Katie Gets Stuck

That was when Mad Iris thought she'd have a go at Big Burger Man's face. She tried to pull off his nose and ears. That didn't work, so she tried to pull out his hair. This worked a lot better.

"Ow! Yow! You pesky chicken!" Big Burger Man took a step back. Mad Iris banged the toilet lid up and down to show how cross she was.

Big Burger Man took aim with his stun-gun.

"Yeee-hah!" Ross flung himself over the top of the door and landed on Big Burger Man's back. He put his hands over the man's eyes.

Katie jumped up and down on the toilet seat. "Get him, Ross! Go on! Pull his head off!"

CRACK!

The plastic lid broke and Katie's feet vanished into the bowl. Water flew up over the sides. Katie couldn't move. Her feet were wedged in the toilet pan.

Big Burger Man tried to grab Ross with one hand, but Ross held on tight. Mad Iris joined in and began pecking at Big Burger Man's clothes. He was trying to get away from her, with Ross still holding on tight. He backed out into the corridor.

"GET OFF!" he yelled at Ross.

He dropped his gun, pulled Ross off his back and threw him down on the floor.

"Now I'll get that bird!" hissed Big Burger Man. "Where's my gun?"

Mad Iris had it. The ostrich liked big, shiny things. She kicked the gun around

with her feet. She pecked it with her beak.
And that was when it went off. *Bing!*

A little stun-dart shot out and stuck in
Big Burger Man's leg.

"You—!" was all he could say before he
fell to the ground.

Ross stood up. "Come on, Katie, we can't
stay here. The others must have heard us by
now. We'll hide upstairs."

Katie's face was white. "I can't move," she said. "My feet are stuck. Take Mad Iris and go before the others get here. I'll be OK. Go on, go, go. GO!"

Ross looked at her for a second and then nodded. He pulled Mad Iris out into the corridor and dashed upstairs.

She ran after him. Somehow she understood that Ross was on her side. In fact, Ross was her only hope now.

Ross looked wildly around for somewhere to hide. He heard footsteps and voices below. The only door up here led on to the school's flat roof. No-one was allowed onto that roof. It was much too great a risk.

"There they are!" cried one of the men. Ross began to panic. What could he do now? Mad Iris gazed all around her. What was that big, red, shiny thing on the wall? It looked good to eat! Mad Iris pecked it. Hard.

Clang-a-lang-a-lang-a-lang!!

Alarms went off all around the school.
Water rained down everywhere. Mad Iris
had set off the fire alarm and water
sprinklers.

The men in black moved back a bit. They
were wet all over. Ross opened the door
onto the flat roof and pushed the ostrich
through. Then he shut the door behind
them.

They stood on a big, flat, empty space.
There was nowhere to hide. They were all
alone on top of the school. Ross looked over
the edge. The other children seemed miles
away.

Ross stood on the roof with the ostrich,
and he felt alone and helpless and scared.

Then the door was flung open and some dripping wet men marched out onto the roof.

"Game's over, boy! Don't move!" yelled one.

Ross turned to the ostrich at his side. "Fly!" he yelled. "Fly for your life!"

Chapter 7
An Unexpected Surprise

But ostriches can't fly. Mad Iris was scared and she did what ostriches do when they are scared. She hid her head down the back of Ross's shirt.

The men came closer.

"Just keep very still, boy," ordered one of the men. "That bird could hurt you badly."

"She isn't going to hurt me," cried Ross. "You've got guns, you're the ones who are going to hurt us."

"Don't be stupid. Just take one step this way, so we can get a good shot at the chicken."

"She's an ostrich," snapped Ross. He stood between Mad Iris and the men.

The men were getting cross. Ross knew this couldn't last forever. Something would have to happen soon, and it did. Mr Grimble poked his head over the edge of the roof.

While the men had been talking, the fire engine had put up its ladder. Mr Grimble had climbed up and now stepped over the edge and onto the roof.

The game was up. Ross would have to give in now. There was nothing more he could do.

The men in black grinned. "Thank you, sir," their leader said to Mr Grimble. "If you could just get the boy out of our line of fire we'll deal with the chicken right away."

Mr Grimble came up to Ross. He put a hand on his arm and gripped it hard. What awful thing would he do next?

Mr Grimble stared at the five men. "You are not going to do anything to this bird," he said. "You can put down your guns and leave the school at once. I am in charge here and I want you out of here in five minutes."

"But …" began one of the men.

"No buts," Mr Grimble told them. "The ostrich stays here with us."

"But she's our ostrich!" cried the men.

"No, she isn't," smiled Mr Grimble. "I've just bought her for the school. We're going to keep her as our lucky mascot and we're going to look after her. Goodbye!"

The men marched off, looking angry.

Ross looked down from the roof and saw that the whole school was cheering in the playground below. They were yelling and waving their arms.

Mr Grimble, Ross and Mad Iris stood on the roof together. Ross felt madly happy. Mad Iris just felt mad. She undid the laces on Mr Grimble's shoes.

"You must be a good girl," he snapped. "If not I shall ... oh! She's eaten my glasses." Mr Grimble gave a sigh. "Shall we go inside?"

Ross smiled. He thought that was a very good idea.

They were going down the stairs when Ross remembered Katie. What would Mr Grimble say? Perhaps it would be better not to tell him. But Ross couldn't just leave Katie in the boys' toilets.

"I've got to show you something," Ross said as they came to the boys' toilets. Someone was shouting inside.

"Ross! Are you out there? If you leave me here forever, I shall never hold hands with you again!"

Mr Grimble gave Ross an astonished look.

Chapter 8
Ross Makes up his Mind

"That sounds like a girl," Mr Grimble said, and Ross nodded. "Why is there a girl in the boys' toilets?"

"I think you'd better take a look," Ross said, and Mr Grimble went in.

"Ross!" yelled Katie. "If you get me out you can kiss me if you want!"

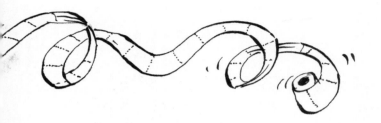

Mr Grimble looked even more astonished. Ross went red.

"Girls!" he said. "What can you do?"

Mr Grimble pushed open the door. Katie still had both feet stuck in the toilet pan. She gave Mr Grimble a pale smile. "Oh! I thought it was Ross."

"So it seems."

"Did you hear what I just said?" Katie asked Mr Grimble.

"About Ross and ...?" Mr Grimble shook his head. "I didn't hear a word," he said. "We'd better get you out, hadn't we?"

It took half an hour to free Katie's feet from the toilet pan. Mad Iris tried to help by pulling the chain several times. She wrapped Mr Grimble in toilet paper. Then, when he got angry and yelled at her to stop, the ostrich put her head down the back of his jacket.

At last, Katie was able to stand on dry ground. Her feet were a bit sore but she was fine. They went out onto the playground, where they were greeted with huge cheers. Mad Iris marched up and down, looking very proud of herself.

Kelly Jessup came over to Ross. She smiled and put a hand on his arm. "You were just *so* brave," she said. "And clever. You can go out with me if you want."

Ross looked across to where Katie was talking to Mad Iris. She had freckles all over her. She was friends with an ostrich. She was mad.

Ross smiled at Kelly. "I'm with her," he said. "And the ostrich."

Problems with a Python

by
Jeremy Strong

Adam's got a problem and it's out of control!
A snake has escaped. It's loose in the school
and it's Adam's fault! Can he find it before
things get wildly out of hand?

You can order *Problems with a Python 4u2read edition* from
our website at www.barringtonstoke.co.uk